Benjay and the Magical P...

A Short

CW01082264

Benjay's Halloween

Dale J. Moore

Published by Northern Amusements, Inc., LaSalle, Ontario.

This is a work of fiction. All of the characters, organizations, and events portrayed in this novel are either products of the author's imagination or are used fictitiously.

Bubbles Book 1.1: Benjay's Halloween / Dale J. Moore - 1st Edition

ISBN 978-1-0689823-0-9

Cover by Dale J. Moore
Edited by Maureen P. Moore
Printed and bound in the United States and/or Canada.

Dedication

To my family and the memories of Halloweens gone by. From bumblebees to pumpkins to princesses to Sonic the Hedgehog and every other costume, it was always fun.

Benjay and the Magical Bubbles

A Story of Wonder
Book One

Danger at Christmas
Book Two

Benjay's Battle
Book Three

Table of Contents

0   Halloween

"Halloween…" Lindsay drew out the word with trembling tones. "The night when ghouls and wart-covered witches haunt the world of the living. The night when no one is safe walking the streets alone." Slowly turning the flashlight upward to illuminate her face in the otherwise dark bedroom, the maneuver scared her younger brother Benjay under his bed sheets, only his eyes and top of his bald head remaining visible. She continued, "The night when kids disappear, never to be seen again!" Benjay dove completely under his covers, the outline shaking in the near darkness.

The bedroom door sprung open, filling the room with light from the upstairs hallway.

"Lindsay Marshall!" her mother exclaimed, looking at the trembling sheets covering her just- turned eight-year-old son. "I've told you that Benjay isn't old enough for your scary stories."

Benjay's head peeked out from under the covers. "It's okay, Mom. I wasn't really scared. I was just pretending to make Lindsay feel good."

Lindsay snorted. "Yeah, right. And your bed shakes like that all by itself."

"That's enough, you two," Mrs. Marshall shushed them. "Halloween's tomorrow. No more storytelling like that. Understood?"

The kids both nodded, though Lindsay fought back a smirk.

"Good. Lindsay, off you go. Let me get Benjay tucked in good night."

"Sure thing, Mom." She stopped in the doorway. "Benjay, I'm sorry if you dream of witches chasing you on their broomsticks or goblins coming out from under your bed in your sleep." She giggled as her mom shot her a glare, then left the room with her flashlight in tow.

"You know her stories are all made-up nonsense, don't you?" Mrs. Marshall asked her son.

"Yeah, sure I do," he said with a quavering voice that showed he wasn't sure.

"Well, I can tell you they don't exist."

"Maybe … " Benjay started, "but last spring you told me bubbles weren't real and couldn't talk."

His mother paused. Her son was correct. He had proven her wrong when the Bubbles indeed proved to be not only real, but could talk, fly, and much more. "You got me there, kiddo. But let's call that an exception. The only exception. Okay?"

"Yes, Mom."

"Good, now you get to bed. You have a doctor's appointment tomorrow morning, remember? They must look at your prosthetic leg because of that issue you've had with the foot not bending properly since the earlier repair."

"Yep, I remember about Prosty's exam." A thought jumped into his head. "Did you finish adjusting my costume?"

"You bet I did. You can try it on tomorrow when we get home from your appointment."

Benjay's face lit up. "I'm going to be the best Super Jet Flying Alien ever – thanks, Mom!"

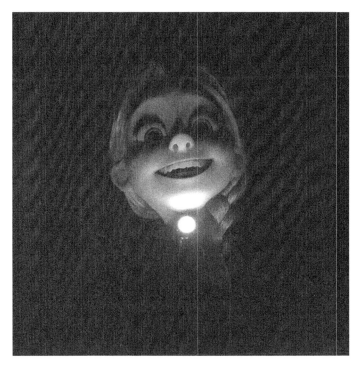

Lindsay using a flashlight to scare Benjay.

1   The Next Day

With the ringing of the afternoon recess bell, Benjay loaded up
his all too heavy backpack and headed toward the front doors of
the school. His mother would be there soon, having taken the
afternoon off work to take him to his doctor's appointment to get
Prosty looked at. As he walked, his prosthetic decided on its own
to bend the foot upwards, making Benjay walk on his heel with
the toes up in the air. It was bothersome, but he'd learned to deal
with it the past few days. Sometimes, he would step on the toes
with his other foot to force the prosthetic in place, but today,
carrying the backpack and not wanting to be late, he lumbered
along. Opening the door, he saw his mother standing in front of
the parked car chatting to the on-duty teacher.

"There's my Super Flying Alien," his mother called out upon sighting him. She leaned over to hug him, then took the weight of the backpack off his shoulders. "Got all your homework assignments?"

"Super *Jet* Flying Alien. Yes, Mom," Benjay replied, trying not to roll his eyes, a habit he'd started picking up from Lindsay.

"Good luck at your appointment," the on-duty teacher called out to them as Mrs. Marshall and Benjay got into the car.

Mrs. Marshall waved, closing the door behind her. She glanced back at her son to ensure he'd properly buckled himself into his booster seat.

As they pulled away from the school, Benjay remembered something from his walk to the bus with Lindsay that morning. "Mom, old lady Williams's cat has gone lost."

"Benjay!" his mother exclaimed. "Please call her Mrs. Williams."

"Yes, Mom," he sheepishly replied, forgetting that Lindsay said not to use that name around Mom and Dad. "Her cat Midnight has gone missing. There are posters on some poles and at the bus stop. He's black as night with a little white teardrop on his forehead."

"She must be worried sick. Midnight is older than you. Black cats can get treated rough at Halloween. Scary stories have painted them as witches' helpers. How about we keep an eye out for him on our way home today? Maybe we'll spot him on our street."

"Thanks, Mom. There's a reward too. That would be nice to get."

"If we find him, we won't be accepting her reward. Good neighbours do favours without expecting rewards or payback."

"Like when Lindsay forgot her bike at the playground and the Reynolds boy returned it?"

"Exactly like that," his mother smiled. "We offered him a reward, but he didn't accept it. Instead, I sent him home with some home-made cookies."

"Home-made cookies are a pretty good reward," beamed Benjay.

"I tell you what. If we find Midnight, I'll make you a batch of home-made cookies. Deal?"

"Deal," Benjay excitedly replied, sitting up tall in his seat.

Pulling into the doctor's office parking lot, Benjay quipped. "I don't know why Dad didn't just oil the ankle mechanism of Prosty. That's what he did when the garage door would stick in the metal tracks. I bet that's all it needs."

"Prosty is an expensive device. Your father was worried he'd ruin it somehow with the wrong oil or getting oil on other sensitive parts."

"I guess that makes sense," Benjay added, unbuckling his seat belt after they came to a stop. "Hopefully, Dr. Miller knows what kind of oil to use."

They entered the almost empty office and had just sat down when the receptionist called Benjay's name. They followed the nurse into waiting room one.

The young, athletic-looking doctor entered the waiting room, partially closing the door behind him. "So, Prosty is giving you some problems, is he?" He smiled at Mrs. Marshall.

"He keeps sticking his toes in the air for no reason," Benjay replied.

"Maybe he just needs a little oil," the doctor answered.

Benjay looked at his mother with a 'told you so' look.

"Let's take Prosty off for a few minutes, okay? It makes it easier to examine him."

Benjay nodded, rolling down the leg housing to gently pull him off.

"Let me see your leg for a second, son. I thought it looked a little red." He examined the stump, looking all around the bottom. "Hmmm," he said a few times as he continued the scan. "I'm going to give you a sample of a cream that will ease the redness down there and provide relief."

"I didn't think it looked infected," Mrs. Marshall replied. "Only a little red."

"You're correct. He's been keeping it very clean. It's likely a little abrasion, perhaps even caused by the foot issue causing him to walk unevenly. Using this cream for a week should clear up the redness and any irritation. We can look at it again in a week if it's not subsiding. Okay?"

Mrs. Marshall and Benjay nodded.

"Good. Now let's look at your friend here." Dr. Miller moved Prosty's joints around, until he was able to replicate the issue. "Ah, there it is," he smiled. "Let me get my magnifying glass out to examine this further." He took a closer look, then grabbed a very small tube, precisely placing a drop on each side of Prosty's ankle. He played around with the foot for several minutes, unable to replicate the issue – at first. Then the ankle locked in place. "Darn it," he said, looking at Benjay. "I guess the little oil isn't going to do the trick."

"I guess it's a good thing my father didn't try to oil it."

"Oh yes, nobody should try to fix these on their own," the doctor responded. "They need to be treated with care, in spite of their sturdy looks."

"What can be done?" his mother asked. "Does Benjay need a new leg?"

"Oh, no. Nothing that rash, I hope," Dr. Miller replied soothingly. "But Prosty does need sending away for examination by the technicians who build them. They are much more skilled than I am."

"How long will that take?" Sophia Marshall asked.

"At least three to four business days, I'm afraid."

"But it's Halloween tonight!" Benjay exclaimed.

"I'm sorry, buddy, but you can't be walking around with Prosty with this going on. Besides, it will give time for your leg to heal a bit." He turned to Benjay's mother. "I can give him a wheelchair, but it's nothing fancy."

Benjay shook his head quickly, with a look of fear on his face.

"They remind him of hospitals, so he's not too crazy about them. Plus, it's very hard for him to move them on his own. He doesn't have the arm strength yet."

"Crutches?" the doctor offered.

"Just some to borrow to get to the car, please. He's got some at home that he can use, right Benjay?"

Benjay nodded, a small amount of relief on his face.

"I know this isn't good timing, Benjay. But Prosty needs fixing right away. You understand?"

"Yes, sir," he nodded.

"Good. Ask Betty up front to schedule a follow-up for a week from today. If Prosty gets back earlier or is delayed, we'll reschedule. I can check that leg when you come back. Have a good Halloween, Benjay." He leaned forward and whispered, "ask Betty for a Halloween treat – she's got some stashed behind the counter." He smiled, giving Benjay a pat on the head.

Poster for the missing cat, Midnight.

2   Back Home

The front door of the Marshall house slammed shut, followed by the thud of Lindsay's backpack.

"You guys are home already!" she said at the sight of her mother and Benjay in the kitchen. After a hug and peck on the head from her mom, Lindsay looked at her younger brother. "You look like someone ate your lunch, or worse, your cookie dessert."

"Benjay got bad news today, didn't you, son?"

"Prosty has been sent to the techitchin for repairs."

Lindsay held back her laugh. "I bet the *technician* will fix him good as new."

"Hope so, but I have to use crutches for a week while he's gone."

Lindsay looked at her mother, knowing what was coming next.

Benjay continued. "How can I be a Super Jet Flying Alien with one leg?" His lower lip came forward producing a major pout. Tears weren't far behind. "I guess I'll stay home with Mom and give out candy,"

"Nonsense, dear," his mother replied. We'll just tuck up your pant leg. Nobody will notice."

"Mom! Of course they'll notice, with me limping along with crutches. The kids already give me weird looks because of my bald head and prosthetic."

"Maybe the parents will feel sorry for you and give you extra candy," Lindsay added, trying to see a bright side.

"I don't want to be felt sorry for. I just want to be a normal kid."

"Okay," Lindsay smiled. "I've got an idea, but we'll need a new costume, if you're okay with that."

"What's this great idea," Benjay sighed as he asked.

"What sometimes has one leg … and wait for it … an eye patch?"

"A pirate!" Benjay exclaimed.

"Yep. I was a pirate a couple of years ago and still have the costume kicking around. We'll just get rid of the girlie touches – like the skirt."

"And I've got a pirate sword that I can use! Thanks, Lindsay. Let's go get my new costume ready."

Mrs. Marshall smiled at her daughter, proud of her problem solving skills.

Getting up from the kitchen table, Benjay filled in Lindsay about the missing cat, and about the reward for finding Midnight, though they would get cookies instead.

"Pirates are good at finding things, like loot, so maybe you'll find Midnight," Lindsay told him as they disappeared upstairs to assemble the new costume.

3   *Another Wrinkle in the Night*

Mrs. Marshall usually arrived home from work around six in the evening, though she tried to sneak out earlier on Halloween. With the afternoon off after Benjay's appointment, she enjoyed having the time to prepare dinner without rushing or re-heating something she'd made the night before. Humming as she put the finishing touches on the main course, she moaned as her phone rang. Fearful of a problem at work, she hesitated to grab the phone. Relenting, she groaned more seeing her husband's number come up.

"Don't tell me you're working late tonight?" she answered the phone.

"I'm truly sorry. A machine more or less short-circuited on the plant floor not twenty minutes ago. We're in crisis mode here, with a couple of workers having minor injuries to tend to. Tell Benjay I'm really, really sorry."

"He's not going to take it well at all. They sent his prosthetic away for repair. The kids are just about to show me the new pirate costume they made for him, since he can't be a Super Alien action figure with one leg."

He ignored the incorrect name for his son's costume. "Maybe you can take him out early, before kids come to our place?"

"That won't work. We have a lot of young kids that come early. I wouldn't want to disappoint them by not being here to hand out candy." She sighed, hearing Randall doing the same on the other end of the line. "Don't worry, dear. I'll figure something out. Just take care of your employees. We'll see you later."

Lindsay came bounding down the stairs, waiting for her brother to follow, though much slower without Prosty. She could hear him hopping, one stair at a time.

Mrs. Marshall wiped her hands with a tea towel, turning to focus on the grand entrance of her pirate son.

"Here he is," Lindsay said. "The menace of the seven seas, slayer of sea monsters, swashbuckler supreme, and finder of gold doubloon-filled treasure chests, Benjay the Bald Buccaneer!"

Benjay entered the room, a pointy pirate hat perched on his bald head. An eye patch covered his left eye, above a drawn-on scar on his cheek. He wore Lindsay's puffy pirate shirt, which hung down past his waist. His left pant leg folded and pinned back, he leaned on his crutch with one arm while wielding a plastic sword in the other.

"Oh my," Mrs. Marshall stated. "He looks amazing, Lindsay. Thank you!" She grabbed her phone, getting Benjay to pose for a few pictures. "Okay, let's eat."

"What about Dad?" Lindsay asked.

"Your father has an emergency at work. Some workers got injured. He is responsible to make sure they get the care they need." She motioned for the kids to sit down as she moved plates and bowls of hot food to the table, then sat down.

After a moment of prayer, the kids didn't hesitate to load up their plates. With the first mouthful of food, Benjay asked, "Who's taking me out trick or treating? Wasn't Dad doing that this year?"

"I guess I could call my folks. Grandpa Joe can walk you around."

Lindsay spit out part of her food. "No. No. No. That won't work. Don't you remember when Grandpa Joe took me out two years ago? You were at the hospital with Benjay. He stopped at every house and talked to the parents for ten minutes. I only trick or treated at six houses before he was tired and brought me home. You can't do that to Benjay when he's missed the last couple of years."

30

"Point noted." Her mother paused, thinking. "Okay, I'll take Benjay out. Grandpa can give out the candy here."

"You can't do that to me again either! Last year I went out with Marcia and her mom. When we came back down the street, there was a line up down our sidewalk all the way to the street. Grandpa Joe was asking every kid to answer Halloween trivia before he'd give them candy. My friends made such fun of me the next day it was brutal!"

"I see," Mrs. Marshall sighed. She looked at her son. "Any friends that you can go trick or treating with them and their parents?"

Benjay looked at the ground. "No." He whispered, "I don't really have any friends since…" his voice trailed off.

Feeling for her brother, Lindsay chimed in. "I'll take him. We'll go early and I'll join up with Marcia on her way back down our street."

"I'm not sure, Lindsay. You're still kind of young. What about Benjay joining you and Marcia instead?"

"We go too late. He'll be dragging his sorry little butt after three or four houses and slow us down."

Mrs. Marshall sighed. "Okay, but just up this side of the street to the corner, and back down the other side. That's it. Deal?"

"Deal!" both kids hollered out.

Grandpa Joe asking trick-or-treaters Halloween Trivia.

4   Final Preparations

Mrs. Marshall stood over Lindsay, applying the final touches to her daughter's witch makeup. "How's that look, dear?" she asked, leaning back to give her work the once over.

Lindsay looked in the mirror in the bathroom, slowly turning her face side to side to get the whole effect. "You nailed it, Mom. I look hideous!"

"I guess that's a compliment," Mrs. Marshall laughed. "Are you sure the nose isn't too long? It looks too long."

"Maybe, but it's a good look," Lindsay grinned. "I'm going to get my flashlight to give Benjay a little scare."

"Take it easy on him tonight. He's had a rough day."

"You're too protective of him sometimes, you know that, right?"

Her mother sighed. "It's what parents do."

"Not some of the other parents that I know. They let their kids do whatever they want, whenever they want." She looked at her mother. "Before you give me a lecture, I was going to say those are the kids that are always getting into trouble at school. So, keep overprotecting away, but maybe ease up on Benjay a bit at times. You can't do everything for him."

Her mother sighed again, this time at how mature her daughter was becoming.

"We will be perfectly safe trick or treating," Lindsay added, standing up. "It will still be daylight when we leave, and we'll only be gone thirty minutes."

"I know," her mother replied. "I need the two of you downstairs for pictures before you leave. You know the

Grandmas will want to see you decked out since you're not going over there anymore for Halloween."

Mrs. Marshall had the candy out in big bowls on a table at the doorway, ready to give out to the soon-arriving superheroes, princesses, and monsters. One bowl was bursting at the seams with small chocolate bars, a second with bags of chips, and a third with assorted licorice packages. She always had extra, which she and Randall would get into once they'd shut off the outside lights for Halloween handout hunters. The kids stood peacefully beside each other; not always the case when picture time happened. They both looked great, tolerating a few retakes.

"Can we go yet?" Benjay whined, tired of the photoshoot.

"I guess that will do," his mother replied, putting her phone down. "You remember the rules, Benjay?"

"Yes, Mother. Don't leave Lindsay's side. No running, especially across the street. No cutting across lawns and say 'please' and 'thank you' to everyone, even if they give me yucky candy."

"I think you got it," his mother smiled. "Take care of your little brother," she added, looking at her daughter, noting that the twelve-year-old appeared to have grown even more. Maybe she'd snuck some heels under that long witch's dress.

"Okay, Mom. See you soon!" Lindsay said before her mother could throw out any more rules, hauling Benjay out the door with her. As they walked down the sidewalk, Lindsay swore she heard her mother's camera click, and a sniffling sob of sadness.

Lindsay dressed up as a witch.

5   *Trick or Treat!*

Walking down the sidewalk, Benjay noticed that neighbours had inflated the Halloween characters on their front lawns. Some looked funny. Some were kind of scary. The scariest house was the Mitchells' two-storey at the corner. They had a twelve-foot tall skeleton hovering over tombstones and graves with disembodied hands moving on the ground. He was happy it was still daylight. They'd driven by it a couple of times at night. It totally creeped him out.

"Okay, Benjay, first house. Do you need me to hold your bag, since you've got a crutch in one hand and a sword in the other?"

"I can handle. Besides, when you helped carry my basket at Easter you took a cut of my candy. Candy tax you called it."

She laughed. "No candy tax, this time, little bro."

They got to the front door and hollered 'trick or treat.' The door opened and the sixteen-year-old boy that answered dumped a handful of candy in each bag.

"Thank you!" Benjay yelled out.

The kid nodded, closing the door without saying a word.

Lindsay shrugged. "One down. Let's go."

After a few more houses, Benjay asked for a break. The crutch was digging into his armpit a bit. Lindsay groaned a bit, but the bus stop was right there so they sat down. She rummaged through her candy. "I see a couple things already that I'm going to want to trade."

"We'll see," Benjay replied. "I'm not sure I'll want to part with anything, especially those Swedish berries that you are ogling."

"Don't sweat it. Marcie doesn't like them, so I can get any of hers by trade. Are you about ready to go again? It's starting to get dark."

"Sure," he answered, maneuvering his crutch to stand. As he turned, he screamed.

"What is it?" Lindsay asked, concerned he'd hurt himself.

"Midnight! Mrs. Williams's cat. See – over there!"

Lindsay turned to see the cat hiding near an inflated dragon with two heads on the lawn of the next house on their tour. The dragon heads moved around vigorously in the slight breeze. "Stay still, little bro. I'm going over to get him."

"Careful," he whispered. "I think it still has its claws."

"Thanks for the heads up." She hiked up her long witch dress, edging toward the cat. She whispered to herself, "Come on, Midnight. Black cats are supposed to like witches." She got within two feet of the scared cat, when it suddenly darted toward the inflated dragon. Lindsay lunged at it, missing the shifty cat and plowing face first into the large inflatable, then bouncing backward onto her butt.

"You let it get away!" Benjay exclaimed.

Lindsay got up, dusting bits of fallen leaves off her dress. As she stood, Benjay laughed.

"What's so funny?"

"Your nose. It's all scrunched up."

Lindsay felt it. "I bet it looks scarier now, right?"

Benjay nodded.

"Cool," she replied. "Where did the cat go?"

"Don't know," he responded, shaking his head.

"Alright," she said. "Let's do this house, since we're already near the door."

They completed the houses on their side of the street and carefully crossed over. Benjay was still sore but soldiered on. On the other side of the street, he stopped. They stood right in front of the Mitchells' large house – in the dark. Their lights spookily moved around the yard. Eerie groaning and moaning sounds came from hidden speakers on the ground.

"Er, can we skip this house?" Benjay asked. "My leg is getting sore."

"Is it really your leg, or perhaps," she pinched her finger and thumb together, "you're just a little bit scared?" She added a witch cackle for effect.

Benjay jumped.

"Yes," he quivered. Just as quickly he forgot his fear. "Midnight! She's on the lawn, on the grave in front of that big tombstone."

Lindsay looked over, staring down the lost cat. "I can get him this time," she said confidently. "You have to come with me though so we can corner him."

"Okay," Benay replied. "Just tell me what to do and I'll try."

She cautiously walked up the sidewalk, then off the path onto the grass. Lindsay motioned to Benjay to go to the grass on the other side of the tombstone. The cat backed up against the large tombstone, swivelling its head to eye both children. Closing in, Lindsay edged forward, ready to take a quick step toward the cat. Unfortunately, she tripped on her long dress, then on one of the animated hands sticking out of the ground. She face-planted on the grave. Benjay, meanwhile, had closed in from the other side. When Lindsay dove to the ground, the cat leapt away from her, toward Benjay. He bent down to pick up the wayward feline, but it shot quickly between his leg and his crutch, clipping the wooden support as she scurried by. The crutch flew out of Benjay's arm toward the giant skeleton. In the air, the crutch took out one of the lines that tethered the skeleton in place. Benjay fell onto his back on the ground, looking up at the huge collection of bones, which began to teeter with one of its two support lines gone. He heard a snap and watched the other support line whip through the air, striking the skeleton's chest. The entire bone structure began to tilt backwards, before suddenly tipping forward, plunging toward Benjay lying on the ground. The young boy crossed his arms in front of his face in defence as the skeleton plummeted toward his small body. He closed his eyes and heard a violent crash. Peeking out from his eye without the patch, he could see the skeleton lying above him, but not touching him. The arms of the creature had prevented it from crushing him, instead trapping him in a cage of pretend bones. Lying still, he felt something rub up against his face. Something soft. Something furry. Midnight rubbed against him, then cuddled up in his right arm, safe from danger.

Mr. Mitchell came running out of the house, asking if the kids were okay, apologizing for the accident. He helped Lindsay to her feet. The two of them lifted the skeleton up high enough that Benjay, still holding Midnight, could crawl out.

Benjay and Midnight under the giant skeleton.

6 The End

"Trick or Treat!"

Kids hollered in front of the Marshalls' front door. Opening the door, Mrs. Marshall looked out to see her children standing there, looking like they'd been rolling around in a stack of hay. They stood there grinning ear to ear.

"What in the world happened to you two?"

"We saved Midnight!" Lindsay exclaimed. "It wasn't easy, but he is safe at home with Mrs. Williams."

"Look what she gave us!" Benjay exclaimed. He held out a brand new box of shortbread cookies.

"And she gave us money," Lindsay added. She looked at Benjay, waiting for her mother to respond.

"Lindsay, you know…"

Her daughter cut her off. "She gave us money, which we told her we were going to donate to the local animal shelter. She wouldn't take no for an answer, so I came up with a solution."

"Well, well," their mother said. "I'm so proud of you two. Your father will be too." She looked again at Lindsay. "Do you want me to help you tidy up, so you can join your friends?"

"Nah, I think I'm good for tonight. Mr. Mitchell gave us a bunch of candy – I'll explain later – so I've got enough. Besides, Benjay says you're baking us home-made cookies for rescuing Midnight."

"A deal is a deal," she smiled, with a little tear creeping out. "Let's get you cleaned up and we'll go through your candy while the oven heats."

Review reminder

If you enjoyed this novel, please spread the word!

I appreciate every honest review of my work. Please take a few moments to provide a review.

Amazon link:

http://www.amazon.com/review/create-review?&asin=B0DHH9TB1Q

For an independent author and publisher, this is the best advertising that I can receive.

Thank you,

Dale J. Moore

Didn't Start with Book 1?

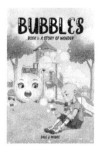

Book 1: A Story of Wonder

A boy and his family, magical creatures with special abilities, and environmental crooks.

What if your new best friend was a Bubble – one that talked and flew? How would you get anyone, especially your parents, to believe you?

Seven-year-old Benjay Marshall wishes people treated him normally. He feels normal; he's just missing part of his leg after dealing with cancer. Fueled by an overactive imagination and a humourous way of expressing himself, Benjay's life takes an extraordinary turn due to a chance encounter with a magical Bubble. As he learns more about the Bubbles, the more he realizes his family will think he's simply spinning another tall tale.

With his father in grave danger from crooks sabotaging his environmental project, how does Benjay make his family trust that Bubbles are not only real, but are possibly the *only* chance to save the day?

An uplifting children's adventure
Bubbles 1: A Story of Wonder is a page-turner, exhibiting healthy doses of humour, wonder, and mayhem along the way. Sure to be enjoyed by both boys and girls.

Book 2: Danger at Christmas

A human boy, a magical Bubble girl, and lives in danger! How far would *you* go to save someone close?

Eight-year-old Benjay Marshall is back for another adventure with the Bubbles!

Having missed Christmas battling cancer the past two years, Benjay is excited to celebrate all the holiday traditions with his family. Happy Christmas activities take a perilous turn with a robbery at the century-old bank where Benjay's mother works.

Benjay's new Bubble friend Peepers has a terrible feeling that her human friend is in danger. Her fears intensify with the ominous vision from a visiting Elder. With a secret motive, the Bubble Elders launch a mission to verify the vision. Peepers and her older brother Fret leave to investigate the curious vision, not knowing the danger they will encounter. All they know are their orders: keep Benjay safe.

Stopping the robbers seems like a monumental task for an eight-year-old boy with a prosthetic leg and his clever twelve-year-old sister. Can Benjay and Lindsay foil the robbery? Can they rescue their mother? Will the Bubbles be able to help?

Book 3: Benjay's Battle

A devious doctor, a secret laboratory, and a boy in a fight against time. And of course, magical Bubbles!

Benjay faces the biggest challenge of his young life. His magical Bubble friend Peepers has no idea of the danger that lies ahead as she breaks the rules to help her human friend. It's the kind of danger that could impact all Bubbles. Mysterious events unfold, including unexplained improvements in Benjay's condition and strange dreams of a woman who may be more than she appears. Join Benjay and Peepers as they face peril in their latest magical adventure!

Benjay's Battle is a fast-paced adventure that blends elements of fantasy, science fiction, and mystery while exploring themes of friendship, curiosity, and hope in the face of adversity.

Printed in Great Britain
by Amazon

49461429R00030